For Kai

PANDA DEMICK

This is a work of fiction. Any resemblance to actual pandas, elephants, lions, eagles, sparrows, giraffes, camels, whales, toucans, koalas, frogs, sea turtles, hippopotami, bees, ladybugs, ants, sloths, flamingos, cats, dogs, frogs, and loving humans, is entirely on purpose.

Written in loving memory of those lost worldwide to COVID-19.

ISBN: 978-1-7356114-1-9
Library of Congress Control Number: 2020920492

PANDA DEMICK

STORY BY **JOHN SHAY**

ILLUSTRATIONS BY **JENNY ZANDONA**

PANDA DEMICK

ITSY BITSY PUBLISHING LLC, SEATTLE, WASHINGTON

Panda Demick lived in a big animal park with his animal friends. Being a panda, he absolutely loved doing panda things like somersaults, climbing trees, and eating.

He especially liked snacking on the fresh bamboo that grew throughout the park.

Although Demick looked like other pandas and played like other pandas, Demick could do something that no other panda has ever been able to do before.

Demick could talk to other animals.

He could talk to itsy-bitsy friends like Ant, Bee, and Ladybug.

Bee told him about collecting flower
nectar and turning it into sweet honey.

Demick could talk to little friends like Dog, Cat, Sea Turtle and Eagle.

His favorite stories were the ones Eagle told about soaring high in the sky over majestic mountains.

Demick also enjoyed talking to big friends like Camel,
Lion, Elephant, and Giraffe.

He heard stories about even bigger friends who sang beautiful songs in the deep oceans.

Demick could even talk to people. Big
people were almost always too busy,
but little people loved to talk to Demick.

One day, little people started telling Demick sad stories about animals living outside the park.

He learned that some Bees were not feeling well after collecting nectar from flowers hurt by pollution.

And an Eagle was injured when he flew into a mountain covered by dirty, smoggy air.

He also heard stories about how Whales were
in danger from trash and noise in the oceans.

These stories were so sad
that Demick started to cry.

When Demick's friends saw how sad he was,
they too started to cry.

They worried for all the animals struggling to live in a world where nature was not being taken care of.

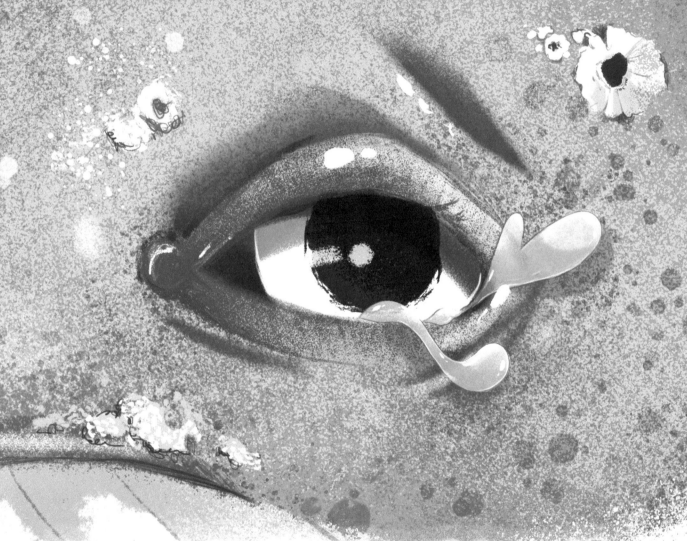

But it wasn't just the animals in the park that were sad. The sadness was felt all around the world and lasted a long time.

During the sadness something else arrived...
Corona, by far the tiniest being that Demick had ever met.

Although Demick could talk to Corona, Corona was so tiny that Demick had to imagine what Corona looked like.

Corona told Demick "With your help, the world can heal. But it has to change. And you will change too."

Demick learned that, to stay safe, everyone needed to stay at home more and start wearing masks in public.

So, he told his big friends, and his little friends, and even his itsy-bitsy friends.

And the whole world slowed down.

As the world slowed down, people had time to remember things.
They remembered big things and little things.

And they remembered that it's the itsy-bitsy things that make them truly happy.

Things like family, and being outdoors, and reading beloved books about purple crayons, hungry caterpillars, and wild things.

Pollution and noise started to go away. Instead of driving cars, people walked and rode bicycles. They flew kites and explored mountains and forests they had never seen before.

At the animal park, visitors planted glorious flower beds. Bee rejoiced by making everyone fresh honey for their morning toast.

And people everywhere started to seek even BIGGER changes to take care of nature and help protect the world we love.

Although it took a while, Corona was right, the world could change...

... and so could Demick.

THE END

... or perhaps a new beginning.

John Shay is a retired Earth scientist and high tech entrepreneur living in Seattle, Washington with his oceanographer wife, Joan. When he's not drawing or writing, he can be found rebuilding their century-old farm house or tending to his beloved fruit trees and raspberries. The birth of his grandson at the beginning of the COVID-19 pandemic inspired him to write the story of Panda Demick.

Jenny Zandona is an illustrator specializing in children's literature. Having grown up in the pacific northwest, Jenny finds inspiration in the ever awe-inspiring beauty of nature, where the day-to-day is a phenomenal sensory expedition. She enjoys swimming, sweets, and morning coffees with her husband, dog, and cat; James, Crow, and Tama, in their too-small-for-four-creatures bed.

CPSIA information can be obtained
at www.ICGtesting.com
Printed in the USA
BVHW020808161120
593408BV00009B/37